THE STORM DRA...

DRAGON GIRLS

Hana the Thunder Dragon

Maddy Mara

DRAGON GIRLS

Hana the Thunder Dragon

by Maddy Mara

Scholastic Inc.

Copyright © 2024 by Maddy Mara

Illustrations by Barbara Szepesi Szucs, copyright © 2024 by Scholastic Inc.

All rights reserved. Published by Scholastic Inc., *Publishers since 1920.* SCHOLASTIC and associated logos are trademarks and/or registered trademarks of Scholastic Inc.

The publisher does not have any control over and does not assume any responsibility for author or third-party websites or their content.

No part of this publication may be reproduced, stored in a retrieval system, or transmitted in any form or by any means, electronic, mechanical, photocopying, recording, or otherwise, without written permission of the publisher. For information regarding permission, write to Scholastic Inc., Attention: Permissions Department, 557 Broadway, New York, NY 10012.

This book is a work of fiction. Names, characters, places, and incidents are either the product of the author's imagination or are used fictitiously, and any resemblance to actual persons, living or dead, business establishments, events, or locales is entirely coincidental.

ISBN 978-1-339-01988-8

10 9 8 7 6 5 4 3 2 1   24 25 26 27 28

Printed in the U.S.A.   40

First printing 2024

Book design by Cassy Price

Hana ran to the front of the banquet hall and pushed aside the curtains. The big windows looked out onto a beautiful garden. Today was her grandma's eightieth birthday. People were coming from all over the country to celebrate. Hana's family was huge and she loved everyone in it.

But there was one person in particular she couldn't wait to see: her cousin Zora.

"Is she here yet?"

Hana jumped, then turned to see her twin sister, Mina.

"I never hear you coming!" Hana laughed. "Then in a flash, you're there."

Her sister smiled. "I definitely don't have that problem with you. I can hear you from a hundred miles away!"

People always said Hana and Mina didn't seem like twins. They looked different, for one thing. Their personalities were very different, too.

Hana loved talking with everyone she met, and somehow, noise just seemed to burst out of her. When they'd chosen an instrument to learn at school, Hana didn't think twice. She HAD to learn the drums!

Mina, on the other hand, had chosen the flute. She was much quieter, but she was also a bright spark. Mina always knew what to do when a problem struck.

But there were lots of things they both loved. Music. Gaming. Their cousin Zora. She was cool and calm, and really fun. The three girls often met in online worlds and played together. But they only saw each other in real life a few times a year.

Mina stood beside Hana and looked out the window.

"A storm is on the way," Mina said.

Hana nodded. Normally, the twins loved storms. There was something so exciting about them. But today, the timing was terrible. A storm could slow down Zora's family.

"She'll be here soon," Hana said. "Hopefully she'll beat the weather."

"Hana? Mina? Where are you? Come here so I can finally do your hair!"

The twins exchanged a look. This was another thing they shared: a hatred of getting their hair done. All day they'd been avoiding their mom, who was determined to give them French braids.

"I want you to look nice and neat for your grandma," she kept saying.

But the girls liked their hair being free!

"Let's split up," whispered Hana. "We've got a better chance of escaping that way."

Mina gave Hana a mischievous smile. "Good idea. You should go somewhere noisy, though. Otherwise Mom will find you instantly!"

Mina dashed off as quickly and silently as she'd arrived.

Hana looked around. Where could she hide? People were bustling around, getting everything ready for dinner. Maybe she could hide under one of the tables? No, too boring! Could she sneak into the kitchen? That was bound to be noisy. But she knew she'd get in the way.

The garden! Her mom couldn't possibly hear her out there. Even better, she'd be there when Zora arrived. Hana glanced through the window at the thick gray storm clouds. She saw a flash of lightning. Several seconds later, thunder rumbled. The storm was still a long way off.

"Girls! Where ARE you?" Her mom sounded closer, and grumpier.

If Hana was going to avoid hair torture, she had to escape now!

As quietly as she could, Hana dashed over to the main entrance. The glass doors automatically slid open. She was going to get outside without making a single sound!

Hana glanced over her shoulder. Where was her mom? She couldn't see her. But she also didn't see the stand of brochures next to the door. With a loud crash, Hana knocked over the stand, sending brochures flying.

It felt like everyone in the whole lobby froze and looked at her.

Her heart pounding, Hana leapt over the mess and ran out the door. Once outside, she dashed across the smooth lawn and ducked under the foliage of a huge weeping willow tree.

She collapsed to the ground, half groaning, half laughing. Why did things like that always happen to her? She just could NOT be quiet!

There was another flash of lightning and rumble of thunder. They were closer together this time. Hana stood up and brushed off her knees.

She knew she had to go back inside. She couldn't leave that mess at the entrance. Her mom would find her, and she'd have tight, painful braids put in.

But then Hana heard singing.

Magic Forest, Magic Forest, come explore...

Hana knew that a band was going to play at her grandma's party. But that wasn't until after dinner. Maybe the musicians were warming up? She heard the song again.

Magic Forest, Magic Forest, come explore...

The singing wasn't coming from the banquet hall. It was coming from somewhere in the garden!

Once again, the thunder boomed. The wind

picked up, rustling the long, drooping branches of the willow tree.

Hana's heart began to beat very fast. She had a feeling that something extraordinary was about to happen. The wind grew stronger, blowing her hair in all directions.

Again, she heard the song. This time it seemed to be riding on the wind itself.

Magic Forest, Magic Forest, come explore.
Magic Forest, Magic Forest, hear my roar!

There was a flash of light, an extremely loud crack of thunder, and then everything went black.

Hana blinked, letting her eyes adjust to the gloom. Thunder rolled again. But it sounded different this time. Was it closer or farther away? Hana couldn't tell.

Light filtered through the willow branches. Except—how odd!—the tree had changed. It was covered in sweet-smelling purple flowers. Surely they hadn't been there a moment ago?

Something strange was going on. The light grew brighter as Hana pushed her way through the leaves. She stopped in surprise. The neat and orderly garden around the banquet hall had vanished. In its place was a wild forest. Tall trees with rough bark stretched toward the sky. The smooth lawn had been replaced by mossy rocks and colorful shrubbery.

A little creature hurried past. The animal looked like a rabbit...but it had a neon-pink tail.

Hana blinked again. *I'll go and find Mina*, she decided. Her twin would figure out what was going on. Mina was lightning fast at solving mysteries.

Then Hana noticed two things. Two very *impossible* things.

The first was that the entire banquet hall had vanished. There was no sign of it at all!

The second was that her legs had disappeared. Well, not *disappeared* exactly. But they had changed. A lot! Her normal legs had been replaced with powerful limbs covered in gleaming scales. The new shoes Hana's mom had bought her for the party had also vanished. Now her feet were huge paws with sharp claws.

Mina and Zora always teased Hana that

when she got excited or frustrated, she would roar. Now Hana opened her mouth, and the sound that she made was most definitely a roar! It felt amazing.

"Am I dreaming?" she wondered aloud.

"If you're dreaming, then I must be, too," said a growly voice.

A fluffy bear cub strolled toward her.

"Um, did you just speak?" Hana asked. She was feeling a little dazed. There was a lot of strange stuff happening!

The bear cub climbed onto a nearby rock. "Technically it's more like growling than speaking," the cub said cheerfully. "But yes, I did." He had a surprisingly deep voice for such

a cute little thing. "I'm Beebi, by the way. You must be Hana. Tell me, have you tried out your wings yet?"

"I have wings?" Hana looked over her shoulder. Sure enough, a magnificent pair of wings sprouted from her back! She looked at Beebi. A few minutes ago, asking an animal a question would have seemed weird. But now it seemed perfectly normal. "What exactly am I?"

"You're a Storm Dragon," Beebi said. "That's why you have a storm cloud on your forehead."

Hana grinned. She somehow *felt* like a dragon—strong and full of power. It also explained the claws. And Hana loved storms, so that felt doubly right!

Thunder rolled again. The sound seemed to trigger something in Hana. A tickling feeling, like a cough rose inside her.

She opened her mouth and another roar burst out, even louder than the last one. Now that she thought about it, her roars sounded a lot like thunder.

"You've certainly got the roaring part fig-ured out," Beebi commented. "But I guess that makes sense. You're the Thunder Dragon, after all. You have a special connection to loud, powerful sounds."

This made Hana laugh. Her sister and cousin would certainly agree! Suddenly, she felt a little pang. If only Mina and Zora were here to share this amazing adventure with her.

"Give those wings a try," Beebi instructed. "We have places to be."

Hana stretched out her wings and gave them a test flap. The action felt strange, but also perfectly natural. She flapped again, with more force this time. She rose a couple of inches off the ground.

"That's it!" said Beebi. "Try again."

With a few more flaps, Hana lifted higher into the air. She began flying back and forth between the trees. She was doing well until another clap of thunder shook the trees. It was so loud that Hana forgot to flap and plopped back down to the ground. Luckily, she hadn't been flying very high.

Beebi glanced around nervously. "We need to get going," he said. "I think the Chaos Critters have spotted you. I must take you to the Tree Queen right away."

Chaos Critters? Tree Queen? Hana had so many questions! But she could tell that now was not the time to ask them. Beebi was focused on other things.

"Let me jump on your back. I'll guide you to the queen's glade," said Beebi.

Hana crouched low and the bear jumped off the rock and landed right between her wings.

With the corner of her eye, she saw something move. Was it a large rat? A lizard?

Beebi saw it, too. "A Chaos Critter!" he growled. "Come on, time to fly!"

Flapping her wings with all her might, Hana rose high into the air. As she weaved her way between the treetops, the wind felt like a giant, invisible hand trying to push her off course. It was hard enough learning to fly as it was. Having the wind blowing directly into her made it much more difficult!

"What IS this place?" she called to Beebi as yet more thunder crashed above.

"We're in the Magic Forest," Beebi called back.

"It's the most wonderful place in the world. But if you don't help us, the Chaos Queen and her critters will destroy it. So fly, Thunder Dragon! Fly as fast as you can!"

The wind kept blowing as Hana flew between the treetops. It sounded like mean laughter. But even worse were the constant crashes of thunder. Every time the thunder sounded, leaves whirled into the air and branches fell from the trees. Hana noticed something. She'd heard lots of thunder, but she hadn't seen a single flash of lightning yet.

"This is all the Chaos Queen's work," Beebi growled into Hana's ear. "She's messing up the storm patterns. And right now, she's trying everything she can to stop us from getting to the glade."

Hana had no idea who the Chaos Queen was. But she sounded like a bully, and Hana hated bullies. She put her head down and flapped her wings harder than ever, forcing her way through the headwind. Leaves, dust, and branches whirled all around.

"Stop, Hana! We're at the glade!" Beebi called above the noise.

But Hana didn't know HOW to stop yet. She stretched out her talons and grabbed on to a tree trunk. Around and around she whirled, Beebi clinging on tightly. Finally, Hana dropped to the ground and rolled onto a mound of fallen leaves.

Beebi tumbled off her back like a furry ball.

"Sorry about that! Are you okay?" Hana hoped she hadn't hurt her new little friend!

Beebi jumped to his paws, laughing a growly laugh. "I'm fine. You sure are a wild flyer! But you've landed in the perfect place. The force field protecting the glade is right there."

Beebi pointed at a wall of twinkling air.

"I can't go through with you," Beebi continued. "But don't worry, I won't be far away."

The little bear pressed his nose against Hana's dragon snout, then scampered off into the forest.

As thunder boomed, Hana turned to face the shimmering force field. Taking a deep breath, she closed her eyes and pressed through it, feeling a tingle against her scales.

When she opened her eyes again, Hana was in a beautiful garden filled with trees, flowers, and lush grass. Birds sang and brightly colored butterflies fluttered around. Hana could still hear the thunder, but it sounded much softer in here.

"Wow! This place is so—" Hana stopped.

Padding toward her were two dragons!

Hana had never met a dragon before, yet somehow she felt like she knew these amazing creatures. One had a lightning bolt on its forehead, and was looking at Hana curiously.

"Mina?" Hana blurted out. "Is that you?"

The dragon leapt closer, her big eyes filled with wonder. "Hana! I thought I recognized you! Guess who this is!"

The Mina dragon pointed a talon at the third dragon, who had a snowflake on her forehead. The dragon's head was tilted to one side. Her eyes were calm and friendly.

"Zora!" Hana cried.

The three dragon girls wrapped their wings around one another. The cousins had met up

in different forms in a lot of online games. But this was something else.

"Where is the Tree Queen?" asked Hana. "I'm so curious to know who she is and why we're here."

"We haven't seen her," Mina said, "but there's

something special about that tree over there. I can't stop looking at it."

Mina pointed to a majestic tree in the heart of the glade. It had bright green leaves and long, graceful branches. The tree's leaves were rustling. But there was no breeze inside the protected glade.

What was going on?

The branches began to sway. As Hana watched, the tree transformed into an elegant woman. She had a wise and beautiful face, long flowing hair, and wore a mossy green dress.

The figure smiled at the astonished group. "Welcome, Storm Dragons. I am the Tree

Queen, ruler of the Magic Forest. I am so glad you are here. The Magic Forest is in dire need of your help. You have probably noticed the constant thunder."

Mina nodded. "And there's never any lightning."

"Yes, that's really strange," agreed Zora. "And it's so windy."

Hana stepped forward. "It's something to do

with the Chaos Queen, isn't it? Can you tell us who she is?"

The Tree Queen swayed as she spoke. "The Chaos Queen is causing a lot of trouble in the Magic Forest. She loves making everything messy and out of control. Chaos is the source of her strength. The wilder things are, the more powerful she becomes. It seems she's targeting the forest's weather by creating an endless thunderstorm. The noise is too much! It stops the animals from sleeping. They cannot hear each other, so they're getting confused about what sounds to make. It's even affecting me. I cannot remain in human form for very long."

Hana frowned. This Chaos Queen was bad

news! "How does she make it thunder all the time?" she asked.

"We suspect she's done something to the Thunder Maker," the Tree Queen answered.

Just then more thunder boomed, making the ground inside the force field shake. The Tree Queen flickered into tree form for a moment, then back into her human shape.

"The Thunder Maker is an ancient machine," she continued. "It is kept at the Thunder Theater."

Hanna, Mina, and Zora looked at one another. The Thunder Theater? Whatever that was, it sounded amazing!

"This is why I have summoned you three,"

the queen added. "You have a special connection to storms. I am hoping you will outsmart the Chaos Queen."

"Of course we will," Hana replied.

The Tree Queen smiled. "Storm Dragons are known for their bravery. I can see you are no exception, Hana."

Again, the thunder boomed, and the Tree Queen transformed back into a tree. When she regained her human shape, she spoke quickly. "There isn't much time. You three must find the Thunder Theater. It's located in the loudest place in the Magic Forest."

She stretched out a long arm. She was holding a silver object that looked like a type of thermometer. It was dangling from a chain. "Hana, put this around your neck. You are the leader of this quest, and this find-o-meter will help you."

Hana put on the find-o-meter. "Thank you. But what do you mean, the loudest place in the forest?"

The Tree Queen opened her mouth as a massive clap of thunder rippled the glade's force field. She flickered back into a tree. And this time, she did not change back.

The three Storm Dragons turned to one another.

"Well, I guess we need to find this Thunder Maker," Mina said.

"I'm ready," Zora said, her eyes twinkling.

Hana nodded, feeling excited but also a little nervous. The thunder continued to roll outside the force field. "How are you both at flying?"

"We love it!" Mina said.

"It's easy!" Zora added.

Hana laughed. She was not at all surprised. When they played online, the three girls always chose flying avatars. It felt like they'd been training for this moment their whole lives.

Hana flapped her wings and rose into the glade's sweetly scented air. "Then let's go."

In a flash, Mina and Zora whooshed high to join her. Together, they pressed back through the shimmering force field and into the Magic Forest beyond.

The thunder clapped and the trees swayed dangerously.

"Which way to the Thunder Theater, do you

think?" Mina yelled to the others over the noise.

"The Tree Queen said we had to find the loudest place in the forest," Zora yelled back. "I wonder where that is?"

Hana wasn't sure, either. Everywhere was pretty loud right now! Then she remembered the find-o-meter the Tree Queen had given her. The queen had said it would help. But how, exactly?

"Let's fly that way," Hana said, pointing. Whenever she was unsure, she followed her gut instinct.

As they flew, Hana and Mina checked the find-o-meter.

"It looks like the temperature is rising," Mina said. "See the silver line, going higher and higher?"

"But the forest doesn't feel like it's getting warmer," Zora commented.

"Then maybe it's not showing us the temperature," Mina said.

"You're right!" Hana grinned. "I think it's directing us! Maybe it's like that game we loved when we were little. Remember Hot and Cold? The warmer it gets, the closer we are!"

"If that's the case, we're going in the right direction," Mina said.

"I wish we could get out of the wind," Zora said, swooping to avoid clipping a tree with her wing. "It's so hard to fly. And branches falling every time it thunders doesn't help, either."

It was very tough going. The falling branches were worrying Hana as well. What if they couldn't stop the thunder, and the branches kept falling and falling? Would the forest be destroyed?

Just then, a flock of birds flew past, calling to each other in alarm. But they didn't sound like birds. They sounded like wolves. Hana could tell that many things were magical and different in the Magic Forest. But birds sounding like wolves didn't seem right. It was just as the Tree Queen had said.

She checked the find-o-meter. The silver line

was still rising. They must be getting closer to the Thunder Theater. At least, Hana hoped they were.

"Look!" Mina called.

Just visible through a break in the trees was a mountain. Hana's pointy dragon ears tilted forward. Was she imagining it, or was the rumbling coming from the mountain?

As the Dragon Girls watched, a plume of glittering sparks shot from its peak. The sparks lit up the stormy sky like fireworks.

"Is that a volcano?" Zora's voice was full of wonder.

It definitely was a volcano, and it was making a lot of noise.

As often happened, Mina said exactly what was on Hana's mind. "Maybe the Thunder Theater is near the volcano?"

"I think it is," Hana called above the racket. "The silver line on the find-o-meter is near the top now. Let's go check it out."

Hana sped up, Mina and Zora close behind. The rumbling grew louder as they approached.

Hana scanned the area with her powerful dragon vision, searching for the Thunder
Theater. But it was difficult to spot something
she had no idea about. She really hoped this
mysterious place wasn't hidden in the lava
somewhere.

"This way!" called a voice from below.

Hana saw Beebi waving a paw at her. He
began scampering along, crawling over rocks
and leaping across spindly shrubs, leading
them around the volcano's base.

Hana followed the little bear, and Mina
and Zora followed her. Hana checked the
find-o-meter. The silver line was still rising.

"Keep your eyes open," Beebi called in his growly voice. "We're close now."

Just then, Hana saw something very strange. Near the base of the volcano was what appeared to be a cave ... with thick, red velvet curtains over the entrance! Hana blinked. Was she imagining things? But Mina and Zora had seen the curtains, too.

"I bet that's the Thunder Theater," said Zora. "It looks pretty theatrical."

Hana pointed the find-o-meter toward the cave. The silver line surged to the very top.

"That's it!" she whooped.

It was certainly a surprising sight. But she

got the feeling that the Magic Forest was full of surprising things.

The three dragons swooped lower and landed. As they approached the cave, the velvet curtains swished apart. Mina, Zora, and Beebi followed Hana into the gloom beyond.

"I can't see a thing," Mina said.

"I can't, either," said Zora. "How are we going to find the Thunder Maker when it's so dark?"

Before Hana could reply, a beam of light began sweeping the cave. It lit up the rocky walls, revealing moving dials, thermometers, and gadgets with whirling propellers. As the light swept past, Hana saw that it was actually coming from a group of glowing insects.

"Welcome to the Thunder Theater," the bugs called in unison. They had surprisingly powerful voices for such little things. "We are the Flame Flies. We look after this place and protect the Thunder Maker."

The Thunder Maker! That's what they were looking for.

"The Tree Queen sent us here. Can we see the Thunder Maker?" Mina asked.

Once again, Mina had voiced what Hana was about to ask herself.

The Flame Flies buzzed in an uncertain kind of way. "You can," said half the group, flying to the left of the cave.

"But you also can't," said the other half, flying to the right. "Follow us."

Hana looked at her friends in confusion. What in the Magic Forest did they mean? Curious, the Storm Dragons followed the brightly colored flies deeper into the cave.

At the back was a sturdy table. Its legs were carved with twisted vines and leaves. On the table sat a small wooden box, worn with age. It was fastened shut with a brass latch.

"This tiny box is making all that noise?" Hana was surprised.

"Well, *yes*," said half the Flame Flies. They flew to the right.

"But also *no*," said the other half, flying to the left.

Hana glanced at her fellow dragons again, trying not to laugh. Flame Flies had a very strange way of communicating.

"The Thunder Maker isn't working properly," explained the flies, swishing back into a single cluster. "We'll open it and show you."

The glowing mass flew over the wooden box,

beaming their light on it dramatically. When they moved away, the latch was undone and the lid of the box was sliding open.

Hana, Mina, and Zora leaned forward eagerly. What was inside this mysterious thing?

A humming sound came from deep inside the box. Then a handle clicked up on one side. The Dragon Girls jumped with surprise.

"Turn it!" called the Flame Flies, hovering in an excited cluster.

It wasn't easy for Hana to grasp the handle with her big claws. Finally, she managed to pinch it between two talons. She carefully turned the handle and a series of cogs sprang up. Attached to each was a model of a storm cloud. As the cogs turned, the storm clouds whizzed around and around.

"That's so cool!" Hana marveled.

She'd always loved machines. When she was three, she'd taken her grandma's radio apart and *almost* managed to put it back together. This year, she'd built a mechanical solar system for her science project.

"It is," said half the Flame Flies.

"But it also isn't," said the other half.

"What do you mean?" Mina asked.

"It's a marvelous machine, but it isn't working

50

correctly," said the first group of flies. "A vital part of the Thunder Maker is missing: the Thunder Drum. Without it, the clouds don't move to the right beat. And they never stop spinning! They just keep swirling."

"This means that there's never a chance for any other parts of the storm to begin," continued the second group.

"Oh." Zora frowned. "Thunder alone isn't a real storm. You need lightning and rain or snow, too."

The twins agreed.

Hana peered at the machine. It was making a clunking, grinding noise that did not sound good at all.

The flies formed a single group once more. "We don't know how it happened. We were doing what we always do, lighting the theater with our protective glow and searching for intruders. But then there was a terrible screeching noise and hundreds of nasty little creatures scuttled in. They ran around wildly, creating confusion and mess. By the time we managed to shoo them out, the Thunder Drum was gone. And the nonstop thunder sounds have been happening ever since."

Hana, Mina, and Zora exchanged looks. Those nasty little creatures were definitely Chaos Critters!

"Can we help find the Thunder Drum?" Mina suggested.

"No," said the flies. For once, they all agreed. "Thunder Drums fall apart very quickly when they're not protected by the Thunder Maker. Sadly, it will be nothing but dust by now."

"Hmm. Is there any way to get another drum?" Hana asked.

She waited for the bugs to divide into two groups. But this time, they all swirled around as if they weren't sure what to say.

"We don't know!" they admitted in unison. "Nothing like this has ever happened before."

One bug separated itself from the group

and flew over to the dragons. It glowed a little brighter than the rest. "There's only one thing to do," it said. "You must go to the Grizzling Bears."

"Do you mean grizzly bears?" Hana asked.

"Grizzly bears? Never heard of them," said the fly. "It's the Grizzling Bears we need right now. Their cave is connected to the Thunder Theater by a tunnel so we often hear them. They're very loud."

"So, why do we need to go to see these bears?" Mina asked in a small voice.

Hana could tell her twin wasn't all that sure about meeting loud bears. Zora didn't look so sure, either.

"Their forebears created the very first

Thunder Maker. They are gifted craftbears. Only they have the skills to make a new drum."

"The Grizzling Bears are distant cousins of mine," said Beebi, coming up alongside Hana. "They can be moody, but I am sure they'll help you."

Somehow, knowing that the bears were Beebi's cousins made Hana feel more certain about what to do. She turned to her own cousin. "I think we should go."

Zora nodded. "Definitely."

It was only a beat before Mina nodded, too.

Hana gave her twin a quick wing-hug and turned to the Flame Flies. "Which way are the bears?"

The flies flew over to one side of the cave. They formed a ring, lighting up a hole in the floor.

The Storm Dragons approached carefully, Beebi staying close to Hana.

"It looks like a tight fit for a dragon," Zora said doubtfully.

"That's because we don't want the bears getting in here," the flies explained. "Once you squeeze through, the tunnel becomes wider."

A loud clap of thunder filled the air, making the cave walls tremble. The flies zipped back to the Thunder Maker.

The brightest bug jumped on a button. The

cogs and swirling model clouds folded down
and the box slid shut.

The flies then fluttered their wings extra
hard, whooshing the machine up through the
air. Just in time, Hana caught it between her
paws.

"Be careful," said the Flame Flies. "If you
lose this precious machine, the thunder will
continue forever. And the chaos will only get
worse."

Hana gripped the box. She really didn't want
to drop it! She turned to Beebi. "Will you come
with us?" she asked.

Beebi shook his furry head. "But whenever

you need me, I'll be there. I promise." With that, he scampered off.

Once again, the Flame Flies separated into two groups.

"Good luck, Storm Dragons," hummed the first group. "We know you can do this."

"Frankly, we're not sure you can do this," said the second. "But we'll keep all our legs crossed."

Hana, Mina, and Zora wriggled through the hole in the floor. The Flame Flies were right. The tunnel was a little wider once they were through. It wasn't wide enough to fly, but it was just wide enough to roll down! Mina and Zora went first. Hana tucked the Thunder Maker tightly to her chest and wrapped her wings

around herself to protect it. Then she began

rolling down the tunnel at top speed.

"I've always wondered what it's like to be

a bowling ball," she called to Mina and Zora.

"Turns out, it's really fun!"

A soft light illuminated the tunnel, chang-

ing color every now and then. Looking up as

she rolled, Hana saw why. Tiny glowing insects clung to the roof, lighting the way.

Suddenly, Mina, who was up at the front, stopped. Zora tumbled right into her. Hana only just managed to slow herself down in time.

"I heard something," said Mina, her ears up straight.

Hana strained to listen. Sure enough, from up ahead came a strange rumbling. It couldn't be thunder way down here. Maybe it was rocks falling? Or bubbling lava?

"It sounds like ... crying," Zora said. "But not sad crying. More *annoyed* crying. The little boy who lives next door to us makes that noise when he's bored."

"It's grizzling!" Hana realized with a shout of laughter. "We must be close now. Let's crawl on a bit farther."

Moments later, the tunnel widened into a huge cave. And there, lying on fluffy rugs, were three very grumpy-looking bears.

6

Hana jumped up, clutching the Thunder Maker and peering at the bears. In the dim light, they looked brown. Her heart skipped a beat. Brown bears could be very dangerous—at least, back home they were. Maybe it was different in the Magic Forest?

Then one of the bears moved and Hana saw

it wasn't brown at all. It was midnight blue! It had little dots of silvery white in its fur that looked like twinkling stars. Were twinkling blue bears dangerous? Hana had no idea! *But they are Beebi's cousins*, she reminded herself. *And Beebi is lovely.*

She turned toward the bears, who were staring intently at the surprise arrivals. They were easily as big as the Dragon Girls, and their claws looked just as sharp.

"What do you want?" the biggest bear asked. His whiny voice didn't fit with his bulky frame. "You gave us a scare, rolling in here like that."

"Sorry about that," Zora said. "We've come to ask for your help."

All three bears began to grizzle again.

"We don't feeeeeeeel like helping anyone today."

"Helping is boooooooring."

"We're too tiiiiiiiiiiiired to help. The thunder stops us from sleeping."

Hana frowned. She always found it annoying

when humans complained. Complaining bears were annoying, too.

"We're actually here because of the thunder," Zora explained.

If Zora was annoyed by the bears, she didn't show it. Hana took a deep breath. She needed to keep her voice calm and even like her cousin's.

"If you help us, then we'll be able to help you," she said.

Hana swallowed as the three bears moved closer. It was hard not to feel nervous surrounded by such powerful beasts.

But I am also a powerful beast, Hana told herself.

"What do you mean, Dragon Girl?" the middle

bear asked. "We're not really in the mood for visitors right now. We all woke up on the wrong side of the cave today."

Hana held out the Thunder Maker. She turned the little handle and the machine sprang to life, its cogs whirring. Thunder cracked and echoed against the stony walls.

The bears gasped. "The Thunder Maker! We've heard so much about it, but we've never actually seen it. Many moons ago, our fore-bears made the Thunder Drum that powers it."

"We know," said Hana, pleased the bears had finally stopped grizzling.

"But where IS the drum?" asked the smallest bear, sniffing suspiciously at the machine. "It's meant to sit right here. That's what our mother told us. And that's what her mother told her!"

"That's exactly why we're here," Hana said. "Unfortunately, the drum has been destroyed."

"Well, it wasn't us," grumbled one of the bears, beginning to grizzle again. "Why do we always get blamed?"

Hana took another deep, calming breath. She was starting to think ferocious bears might be easier to deal with than these whiny ones.

"No one is blaming you. The Chaos Critters took it. But we do need your help. We've heard that only you know how to make a Thunder Drum," she said.

"We are hoping you'll build us a new one," added Mina.

The bears looked uncertain.

"It's the only way to stop the constant sound of thunder," Zora pointed out in her soothing way.

A loud noise rumbled around the cave. At first Hana thought it was particularly loud thunder. But then she realized it was the bears, all grizzling at once!

"It's not fair! Why do we always have to make new drums?"

Hana was surprised. "When was the last time you were asked to make one?"

"Well…never," admitted the smallest bear (who was also the loudest grizzler). "But our great-great-grandbears had to. And then we had to learn how to make them, just in case. It's very fussy and takes FOREVER."

Hana was losing her patience with these creatures. "Don't you care about what happens to the forest? The thunder vibrations are making branches fall from trees. And the forest sounds are getting messed up, too. The wind sounds like laughing. I heard birds howling like wolves. You might start quacking like ducks if we can't fix the Thunder Maker."

The bears looked at Hana, shocked. "We

cannot allow that to happen!" the largest bear cried. "We are Grizzling Bears, not Quacking Bears. If we don't get a good grizzle in each and every day, we don't feel right at all."

"So will you make a new drum?" Mina asked, her voice full of hope.

"We've already told you the problem with that," said the middle-sized bear. "Thunder Drums take a long time to make."

Hana, Mina, and Zora groaned. This was bad news.

"Unless you just take one of the drums we've already made," said the biggest bear.

"You have spare Thunder Drums?" asked

Hana, hardly daring to believe her ears.

He padded over to a wooden door at the back of the cave and pulled it open.

The Dragon Girls gasped. Stacked inside were hundreds of tiny drums!

"Our parents and grandbears made us prac-
tice," explained the biggest bear. "We've been
making them since we were cubs."

"We've always feared that one day something would happen to the original Thunder
Drum," continued the middle-sized bear.

"Which is why we hate making them so

much. We've made soooooooo many," finished the smallest.

With a flap of her wings, Hana was in front of the cupboard. There were enough drums in there to repair a thousand Thunder Makers. "So, can we take one?"

Hana expected the bears to complain about this, but they were surprisingly upbeat.

"Please do! We have so many."

"The one right at the very top is the best, in my opinion."

"It's good that they're finally useful."

Hana looked at the bears. "Why are you suddenly so cheerful?"

"Oh, we're always grumpy when we wake

up from a nap," one replied. "Once we've had a good grizzle, we feel fine again."

"I wish we'd known that before!" murmured Mina.

Hana was relieved that the bears were now being helpful. But something was bothering her. "How come these drums don't fall apart? I thought they didn't last long out of the Thunder Maker."

"That's only after they've been thunderized," the middle-sized bear explained.

The Storm Dragons looked at each other. *Thunderized?*

"Can you...thunderize one for us?" Hana asked hopefully.

The bears shook their blue heads. "We know how to make the drums, but we cannot thunderize them."

The Storm Dragons sighed. Just when they thought their problems were solved!

"Do you know who can?" Zora asked.

"I'd try the Beat Badgers," said the middle-sized bear. "They have the best drumming skills in the entire Magic Forest."

Hana felt a surge of hope.

"They also have the worst voices," the smallest bear added. "Whatever you do, don't let them sing!"

"Where do we find these badgers?" Mina asked.

"They live near here, in a clearing," said the biggest bear. "But they're often underground at this time of year. You might have trouble finding them."

"We'll figure something out," Mina said confidently.

Hana smiled at her sister. When Mina set her mind to something, she always found a solution.

Zora turned to Hana. "Maybe the find-o-meter can help us."

Mina nodded. "We should hurry."

As if to prove her point, there was a crash of thunder, making everyone jump. Pebbles and earth crumbled from the sides of the cave. The Thunder Maker gave a loud rattle.

"Quickly!" urged the bears. "There's a hidden tunnel behind our drum cupboard. That will get you back into the forest in no time."

It was amazing how different the bears were now. They slid the cupboard wall to one side, revealing a passageway. Hana could smell the plants and flowers of the forest wafting down.

"Just remember," the middle-sized bear said to Hana. "When the tunnel divides in four, you must take the second right. Then at the next fork, take the third left, then the next left, followed by the fourth right. It's very straightforward."

It did not sound at all straightforward to

Hana, but they were in a hurry, so she didn't ask him to repeat it.

"Thanks so much!" she and the other Dragon Girls called.

"No problem!" the bears replied.

Hana pressed the button to close the Thunder Maker and picked it up in one paw. In the other, she held the new Thunder Drum.

"You need to check the find-o-meter, so how about I carry the Thunder Maker?" suggested Mina.

"And I can carry the drum," Zora said.

Hana hesitated. The Tree Queen had put her in charge of this mission. Was it okay to let the others carry these important objects?

We're a team, she reminded herself. *And teams help each other out.*

"Thanks, that will make things much easier." Hana handed the Thunder Maker to her sister and the drum to her cousin. Then, with a flap of her wings, she led the way into the tunnel.

"Come again for a visit," called the bears. "Just make sure it's well after our nap!"

This tunnel was just wide enough for the dragons to fly through. As Hana sped along, she checked the find-o-meter. The silver line was steadily rising. But then something strange happened. A red light on the find-o-meter began to flash.

"Hey, guys," she called to Mina and Zora. "What do you think this—"

But before she could finish, the walls of the tunnel seemed to come alive. From the rippling movement, tiny dark shapes appeared. The horrible sound of high-pitched squeaks echoed.

"Chaos Critters!" Hana yelled. "You guys fly ahead, as fast as you can. I'll try to hold them off!"

She slowed to let Mina and Zora go ahead, holding the precious objects. Up ahead, she saw the tunnel branching off in four different directions.

"Don't forget to take the second—"

Hana's call was cut off by the screeching of another swarm of critters. To Hana's horror, one of them leapt onto her back. It was followed by another, and another. She could feel their little feet scuttling across her. Luckily, her tough scales protected her from their claws. These insects were awful!

Mina and Zora were nowhere in sight. Hana really hoped they'd taken the correct tunnel. She flew down the second one on the right. But then the tunnel forked off again. Hana's heart pounded. She couldn't remember which way to go! The critters swarmed and squeaked all around her.

"This way, Hana!" said a growly voice. "I'll guide you to the surface."

Hana felt relief flood through her. She couldn't have been happier to see Beebi's fuzzy little face.

With an extra-strong flap of her wings, Hana zoomed along the tunnel behind the scampering bear. Had they outpaced the critters? But no, she could feel more of the nasty things leap onto her back.

Hana started shaking and wriggling as hard as she could. This wasn't easy to do while flying at top speed through a tunnel. She twisted this way and that. Many of the critters fell off, but some clung on. She felt her frustration build. She wanted the critters off her. NOW! Then she saw something that made her even more furious. The Chaos Critters had jumped on Beebi! They were biting at his ears and pulling at his fur.

A furious roar burst from her, filling the tunnel and bouncing off its rocky walls. With

surprised squeaks, the Chaos Critters let go of Beebi and scuttled away into the darkness. One last critter dropped off Hana and disappeared. Finally!

"Thanks!" growled Beebi. "And look, we are almost at the surface. Unfortunately, I must leave you now. The Beat Badgers are afraid of bears and won't come near if I am with you. But here is some advice: With all the chaos swirling around at the moment, it's wise not to trust your ears."

Then, after a quick nose rub, the little bear scampered out of view.

Up ahead, Hana saw a circle of daylight. Her heart leapt. Almost there! But then she heard something. It sounded like flames crackling. Hana hovered in the tunnel. She didn't want to fly out into the middle of a raging forest fire. But somehow, the crackling noise didn't sound quite right.

Cautiously, Hana flew on. The crackling grew louder. Now Hana could also hear the wind and booms of thunder. At the end of the tunnel, she stopped and looked out. She couldn't see fire anywhere—in fact, she saw the opposite. There was a wide, fast-moving river!

Hana's ears twitched with surprise. The sound of a raging fire was coming from the flowing water!

This must be the work of the Chaos Queen.

Still, Hana was relieved that there was no real fire. She had too many other things to worry about right now. Like, where were Mina and Zora? She looked around, hoping they'd appear. But no luck. Were they still in the tunnel? Should she fly back and search for them? Maybe they'd been attacked by Chaos Critters!

Hana filled her powerful dragon lungs with air. "Mina! Zora!" she roared over the noise of thunder, swirling winds, and the strange river fire. "Where are you?"

Suddenly, a furry black creature with a white stripe down the center of his nose popped out of a hole. He had golden claws and, most surprisingly, was wearing a green velvet vest.

He scampered over to Hana, eyes wide with alarm. "What are you doing?" he whispered. "Do you want to bring the Chaos Queen and her critters right to us?"

"Sorry," Hana said, letting out an anxious puff of smoke. "I've lost my friends. We have to find the Beat Badgers as quickly as—"

Hana stopped and looked at the creature. "Hang on! Are YOU a Beat Badger?"

The stocky creature smoothed down his vest proudly. "I am indeed. We Beat Badgers are the best drummers in the Magic Forest." His little ears drooped. "Not that we can do any drumming right now. The thunder drowns us out and muddles up the rhythms."

"That's why we've come to you!" Hana said.

The badger looked confused. "Why do you keep saying we? There is only one of you, although you are very large."

"I got separated from the other two Storm Dragons," Hana explained.

"Oh! I've never met a Storm Dragon," said the badger. "But I have met the Treasure Dragons. They weren't as shouty as you."

Hana looked back at the tunnel. There was still no sign of Mina and Zora. *What could have happened to them?*

"The problem is," she continued, "my friends are carrying the objects we need your help with."

"What objects?" asked the badger.

"We have the Thunder Maker," Hana said. "Plus a new Thunder Drum."

"Shh! Not so loud!" warned the badger. But

his eyes lit up. "Do you really have the Thunder Maker? We thought it must be broken because the thunder never stops and the rest of the storm never starts."

"You're right, it's broken," Hana said. "That's why we got a new Thunder Drum from the Grizzling Bears. We're hoping you can thunderize it for us."

The badger dropped to all fours and began thumping the ground with his paws. The earth shook. He was surprisingly powerful for such a small creature!

The trembling grew and grew until Hana wondered if there was going to be an earthquake. Another badger peered out from the bushes to her left. Two more appeared to her right. Before long, Hana was surrounded by Beat Badgers, all dressed in elegant velvet vests.

"What's going on?" they asked the badger in the green vest. "You know drumming attracts those horrible Chaos Critters. And the critters attract the Chaos Queen."

"This is an emergency," explained the badger in the green vest, waving his paws in the air. "This Storm Dragon has lost her friends. And the friends have a new Thunder Drum. They were last seen in that tunnel. We have to find them."

Without another word, the Beat Badgers

turned and disappeared into the tunnel. Hana stretched her wings, ready to follow them. But before she could, there was a tremendous whooshing noise and the badgers popped back out of the tunnel—on the backs of Mina and Zora!

"We found them!" cried a badger in a red vest.

"Actually, we found you!" Mina laughed. She turned to Hana. "Sorry we took so long. We got lost down there with all those complicated twists and turns."

"But we haven't lost the Thunder Maker or the drum!" added Zora as she and Mina landed near Hana.

Mina and Zora placed the precious objects on the ground. The Beat Badgers clustered around as the thunder continued to rumble.

"We must thunderize this drum right away," said the badger in the green vest, picking it up carefully in his golden claws.

"It's risky," muttered the badger in the red vest. "The Chaos Critters will probably hear us."

"There's no other way to fix the Thunder Maker," pointed out a badger wearing a mustard vest. "We have to do it."

The Beat Badgers nodded, and formed a circle around the drum. They began to thump the ground with their sturdy paws, in a slow, steady rhythm. Gradually, the thumping became faster and more complex. The drum began to vibrate.

Hana watched with interest.

"I hope they know what they're doing," Mina whispered, picking up the Thunder Maker.

"So do I," Zora said. "There are a lot of critters

nearby. It wasn't easy to outfly them in the tunnels. They'll feel that thumping for sure."

But Hana felt sure the Beat Badgers knew what they were doing. She flew into the air. She was eager to see what "thunderizing" looked like. She also wanted to keep an eye out for Chaos Critters. From above, she watched as the badgers thumped the ground around the drum. Faster and faster their paws went, until they were little more than a furry blur.

Slowly, the drum began changing from plain white to pink to mauve, and then to the deep purple of a thundercloud.

The drum started making a sound: a steady pulse, like a heartbeat.

"It's working! You've thunderized it!" Hana whooped.

"Of course we have." The badgers looked pleased with themselves. "Let's sing a song of triumph."

The little animals began singing. At least, Hana guessed it was singing. It sounded more like rocks being crushed underfoot.

Then she noticed that the red light on the find-o-meter was flashing. "Danger! Watch out, everyone!" she called. But it was too late. The terrible sound of scuttling claws filled the air.

"Chaos Critters!" the badgers cried. "Run!"

The badgers scattered, tripping over Mina and Zora in their haste. The Thunder Drum was now lying unprotected on the ground. Quickly, Hana swooped down to grab it. She was just in time! Chaos Critters scuttled all over the ground where the drum had just been.

"Nice work, Hana!" cheered Mina, grabbing

the Thunder Maker as she and Zora whooshed into the air after Hana.

The Chaos Critters let out high-pitched screeches of anger. They surged up the trees, trying to reach Hana as she flew back into the air. Some leapt off the trees and landed on her. Hana shivered as she felt the critters' tiny sharp claws on her scales. But she kept calm. She did a quick somersault in the air, and the critters squawked as they streamed off her back.

The Storm Dragons whipped their way through the treetops. Hana thought they'd escape quickly, but the Chaos Critters were surprisingly fast. They streaked along just behind the Dragon Girls, surging up trees and jumping easily from one to the next. With their gleaming claws and high-pitched squeaking, they were truly horrible.

"We've got to get away from them!" Hana called. "Top speed, everyone."

The Dragon Girls shot ahead, trying to lose the critters. But they stayed close behind—no matter how fast the girls flew or how many turns they made.

Hana's heart pounded with the effort. The Thunder Maker was still not complete. They needed to get away from these pesky critters so they could put the new drum into the machine and get it working again.

A worry circled Hana's mind. *Would they be able do it?* She pushed the thought aside. They had to!

The fierce wind picked up leaves and dust, flinging them into the dragons' eyes. Even worse, the wind seemed to be pushing along the Chaos Critters, making them go faster.

Hana gritted her teeth. They had to get away from the chaos.

As she ducked beneath a low-hanging branch, she felt something land on her back. It was too heavy to be a Chaos Critter. Looking over her shoulder, Hana was relieved to see Beebi!

"Go above the tree line," the little bear urged. "The critters can't reach you up there."

"Higher!" Hana called quickly to her twin and cousin. Flapping hard, she headed upward. She could hear Mina and Zora right behind her—but she could also hear the Chaos Critters scuttling up the trees. She *really* hoped that these beasties hadn't learned how to fly!

Hana surged through the leafy canopy and into the forest air. The Chaos Critters clustered on the topmost branches, waving their claws in fury. They shrieked with frustration. They could go no farther.

But it was not time to celebrate yet. The

Storm Dragons had flown directly into the middle of a storm cloud! Thunder crashed all around. It was so loud that Hana felt a wave of sound slam against her, pushing her sideways.

"Hold on tight, Beebi," she called. She began to spin, tail over snout, through the dark clouds. The thunder rolled again. This time it sounded like it was sneering at her!

"Hana, you've dropped the Thunder Drum!" cried Mina, still clutching the Thunder Maker.

Through the swirling gray cloud, Hana saw the Thunder Drum tumbling down.

"I'll get it!" yelled Zora, diving after the precious object.

But the thunder exploded again, sending Zora spinning off in the wrong direction. Hana gasped. If the drum fell to earth, it would surely break or be destroyed by critters. And it would be all her fault!

Hana flapped her wings with all her might, but the wind and thunder forced her back. Determination rumbled in her belly. Nothing was going to stop them completing this important mission!

A roar exploded from her, far louder than any roar she'd done before. All her life Hana had been told to keep her voice down. To use her indoor voice. Finally, Hana's outdoor voice was needed. And it felt great!

The next time there was a clap of thunder, Hana felt it bounce right off her.

"Your roar is stronger than the thunder!" cried Mina.

"And look! It's pushing the Thunder Drum back up," Zora called, doing a midair loop. Sure enough, the Thunder Drum was spinning in an upward arc. "Do another thunder roar," Zora urged. "And don't hold back!"

Hana grinned. She had no intention of holding back.

Taking in a huge gulp of thunder-charged air, Hana roared again. This time, something even more surprising happened. The storm clouds began parting and a hopeful beam of sunlight shone through.

Looking down, Hana spotted something gleaming as it spun through the sunshine. *The Thunder Drum!* She surged toward it, catching it in her talons.

"You got it!" the others whooped.

Hana flew closer to Zora and Mina. "Can

you both hold the Thunder Maker steady? I'm going to fit the new drum into the maker."

"Do you know how to do it?" asked Zora, reaching over to help Mina hold the machine.

"Nope," Hana admitted. "But I am sure we can figure it out."

Mina and Zora held the Thunder Maker out so Hana could examine it. This wasn't easy when they were all hovering in midair! Plus, Hana still had Beebi balanced on her back.

But hang on ... was that a space in the center of the machine? *Yes!* The drum had to go in there! Carefully, Hana fitted the drum into the gap. Immediately, the drum popped back out of the machine and into the air!

"Oh NO!" yelled Mina and Zora.

"Go, Hana," urged Beebi. "Catch it!"

She darted forward, just managing to catch the flying drum. But what should she do now?

Hana knew it would be easier to try to fit the drum into the machine on the ground. But that was not an option. The Chaos Critters were down there, just waiting to attack and confuse everything. No, the Thunder Maker had to be fixed up here, in the air.

"You can do it, Hana," Mina said, her gleaming tail swishing back and forth as she flew in place.

"You absolutely can," agreed Zora, in her soft, comforting tone. "And we're going to hold this thing steady for as long as you need."

Hana took a breath and tried again. This time, she pushed the drum until she heard a satisfying click. The drum gave a little shiver. Would it stay in place? Hana held out her claws, ready to catch the drum if it decided to fly out again.

This time, the drum stayed put.

"Yay!" cheered Mina.

But still the thunder boomed in its wild, out-of-control way. Zora reached over and turned the machine's little handle. Instantly, the cogs whirred and the model clouds spun.

"Nothing's changed," groaned Hana. "It's still moving in that random way."

Hana's wings were starting to feel heavy. Hovering in the air was tiring. She could see from Mina's and Zora's expressions that they were getting tired, too. Hana was so frustrated with herself. Back in her normal life, she was good at fixing things! Why couldn't she repair this machine?

Hana felt Beebi nuzzling the back of her neck. "You have to make it start yourself," he said. "You're the Thunder Dragon. Use your thunder-force!"

My thunder-force? Hana had never heard of

this. But somehow, she understood what Beebi meant. Filling her lungs with air, Hana let out all her frustration, worry, and determination.

The roar that burst from her wasn't as loud as thunder. It was much, much louder! The leaves on the trees shook. Beebi, still clinging to Hana's back, shook. Even the air around them seemed to shake.

The Thunder Maker gave another click and stopped moving. Hana held her breath. Had she somehow managed to BREAK the Thunder Maker?

The machine let out a gentle whir, and the cogs and little metal storm clouds began to move in a smooth, steady rhythm. The storm clouds each made one full circle and then, when their paths aligned, they stopped.

Instantly, the thundering around the Dragon Girls stopped as well. The remaining clouds melted away, and the sky became a brilliant azure color.

"You fixed it!" cheered Mina and Zora.

"No, we fixed it," Hana said, beaming at her sister and cousin.

"The Thunder Maker feels lighter," Mina commented.

"I guess that's because it's working now," said Zora.

Hana nodded. "Let's take it back to the Thunder Theater."

The Storm Dragons made their way down through the treetops, guided by the find-o-meter. Beebi rode on Hana's back, snuffling delightedly. He clearly enjoyed the feeling of the gentle breeze ruffling his fur.

Hana was also enjoying the flight. Nipping

through the trees was much easier now that the wind had dropped away. There was no sign of the Chaos Critters, either.

"The critters have gone for now," Beebi growled softly in Hana's ear. "They hate it when the sky is blue. But in time, the storm clouds will be back—and so will the critters."

"We'll be ready for them," said Hana. She felt like she was still full of her tremendous roar. The Chaos Critters didn't stand a chance against the Storm Dragons, she was sure of it!

Up ahead was the volcano. The dragons swooped low to land outside the Thunder Theater. Instantly, the velvet curtains swished open and the Flame Flies flew out in a twinkling cloud to greet them.

"Thank you so much for your help, Storm Dragons," they said, guiding the dragons into the cave.

"We're happy we could help," said Hana, placing the fixed Thunder Maker back in its spot and giving it a gentle pat.

The bugs divided into two groups. "Would you like to stay for dinner?" said the first group, flying to the right. "We're doing a flame grill tonight."

"Then again, we do a flame grill every night," said the other group, flying to the left.

Once again, Beebi spoke into Hana's ear. "We must return to the Tree Queen. She wishes to see you before you go home."

So the Storm Dragons declined dinner, and said goodbye to the Flame Flies. They didn't want to keep the Tree Queen waiting!

The flight back to the glade was wonderful. Hana loved the excitement of a storm, but she also loved the feeling in the air once one had passed. Birds twittered, sounding exactly how birds should. And when the dragons flew above the river, Hana was relieved to hear it was now making the correct watery sounds.

Hana was almost sorry when she spotted the shimmering force field. Flying through the forest had been so nice! But she was excited to see the Tree Queen again, too. The group came to a stop at the wall of shimmering air.

Beebi leapt from Hana's back. "Goodbye for now, Storm Dragon," he said, leaning against Hana's leg. "It's been an honor to help you on this quest."

Hana bent low and touched her nose against the bear's. "For me too," she said. "I hope we meet again."

With a final swish of her tail, Hana followed her sister and cousin through the force field and into the glade.

The queen was already in human form. "Great work, Storm Dragons!" She smiled in her warm, woody way. "I have heard wonderful reports of how well you've done in this first quest."

Hana tilted her head. "*First* quest?" she repeated as she returned the find-o-meter to the queen.

The Tree Queen nodded, her leaves fluttering.

"I fear our battle with the Chaos Queen and her critters is not over yet. Will you three return? We're going to need more help restoring order to our precious forest."

The Storm Dragons nodded without a moment of hesitation.

The Tree Queen's smile grew broader. "Then I will send for you again soon. Watch out for a storm—that will be my signal."

The Dragon Girls grinned. Yet another reason to love storms!

The Tree Queen continued. "Now, to send you back to where you came from . . ." Her branches began to sway, releasing a swirling mist. The vapor soon filled the entire glade. Before long,

Hana couldn't see anything but thick mist everywhere she turned.

"Goodbye, Storm Dragons," came the Tree Queen's voice. "I will see you soon."

The mist faded. Hana blinked. She was back under the willow tree in the banquet hall garden!

She peered out between the branches. The stormy sky had cleared and was now the deep blue of early evening. And there was her mom, walking toward her with a hairbrush and a determined look on her face.

"There you are!" her mom said. "I've been looking for you everywhere. Zora has just

arrived. Are you going to let me do your hair before you see her? It's full of leaves!"

Hana laughed and gave her mom a hug. "Sure."

She had, of course, already seen her cousin— but not in human form. She, Mina, and Zora would have plenty to talk about over dinner!

Turn the page for a special sneak peek of

Mina's adventure!

DRAGON GIRLS

Mina the Lightning Dragon

Mina was sitting at the kitchen table on her mom's laptop, playing a game. She smiled as she watched three avatars flying through a lush forest. Mina was the one dressed in silver. The one in black was Hana, her twin sister. In the middle was an avatar wearing purple. That was Zora, the twins' cousin.

The three girls loved spending time together but they didn't get the chance to do so very often. Zora lived on the other side of the country. Just recently the three girls had all attended their grandma's eightieth birthday party. That had been so much fun. But now they wouldn't see each other for months and months.

Luckily, they could still meet up in online games. *Magic Treasure Zone* was one of their favorites. You had to search for hidden treasures while constantly avoiding danger. It was exciting to play and took a lot of skill.

Mina got better each time they played the game. She loved flying through the imaginary world. But the best part about the game was chatting with the others. Right now, Hana was upstairs in their bedroom, on the computer the twins shared. Zora was in her room, thousands of miles away. Even though they were apart, it felt like they were together.

Outside, lightning flashed. Mina typed a message into the game's chat. *There's a storm coming!*

Zora replied. *There's one coming here, too. I just saw lightning.*

Mina felt a tingling in her spine. Of course, it wasn't impossible for there to be a storm in two parts of the country at the same time. It must happen sometimes.

But something else had happened to the cousins recently. Something that definitely didn't happen very often. The three girls had been drawn into a realm called the Magic Forest. And that wasn't even the most exciting part. Once they were there, Mina, Hana, and Zora transformed into magnificent dragons. They weren't just any type of dragon, either. They were Storm Dragons!

Hana was the Thunder Dragon. This made perfect sense to Mina. Her twin was loud and bold. Mina was the Lightning Dragon, but she wasn't sure yet what her special powers are.. In dragon form, Mina had a lightning bolt on her forehead. And everyone always said she was as fast as lightning. But Mina didn't really care what her special power was. Being a Storm Dragon was amazing, no matter what!

Outside, lightning flashed again. This time it lit up the entire night sky.

Whoa! wrote Zora. *We just had a MASSIVE strike here.*

So did we, typed Hana. *Something is going on. I can feel it.*

The tingling up Mina's back grew stronger. The Tree Queen, the ruler of the Magic Forest, had told them they would see a storm when it was time to return to her. The girls had completed one task for the queen, but there was more to be done.

Mina heard the faint hum of a song. Was it coming from the computer?

Magic Forest, Magic Forest, come explore...

Mina's excitement swelled. She'd heard this song just before she went to the Magic Forest last time. Now she was sure of it—they were being called back!

Mina started typing a message. But something odd happened. The keyboard vanished. Mina blinked. The screen was getting bigger and brighter by the second.

Magic Forest, Magic Forest, come explore...

The song grew louder. It came from all around her. Lightning flashed outside and the window flew open. The room filled with swirling wind and the air smelled like ripe mangoes and cinnamon. On the computer, the forest trees stretched up and out of the screen until they surrounded Mina. Now she could hear the rustling of leaves and smell rich forest soil.

Lightning flashed again and the air crackled with electricity. Mina shut her eyes as the sweet-scented wind swirled around her, lifting her out of her seat. From somewhere nearby she heard the final line from the song.

Magic Forest, Magic Forest, hear my roar!

Mina felt herself plop gently back down as the wind died away. But she didn't land on the chair. Beneath her she could feel soft grass.

I'm back in the Magic Forest! she thought, her heart beating fast.

Mina blinked open her eyes. Everything was dark except for a mysterious pale green glow.

The only noise was the faint rustling of the trees.

Something's not right. Mina could feel it in the air.

A strange static noise rose up, crackling louder and louder. A glowing bolt of green ripped across the sky. Lightning! Usually Mina loved lightning. In her opinion, it was the most exciting part of a storm.

But this was no ordinary lightning. It was acid green, for one thing. And rather than making a zigzag across the sky, this lightning traced out a confused, tangled scrawl like a toddler's drawing.

Mina's stomach clenched. Last time they

were in the Magic Forest, there'd been a problem with the thunder. The Chaos Queen and her critters had stolen part of the Thunder Maker. Luckily, Mina, Hana, and Zora had managed to fix it.

"It looks like the Chaos Queen is messing with the lightning now," Mina said aloud.

ABOUT THE AUTHORS

Maddy Mara is the pen name of Australian creative duo Hilary Rogers and Meredith Badger. Hilary and Meredith have been making children's books together for many years. They love dreaming up new ideas and always have lots of projects bubbling away. When not writing, Hilary can be found cooking weird things or going on long walks, often with Meredith. And Meredith can be found teaching English online all around the world or daydreaming about being able to fly. They both currently live in Melbourne, Australia. Their website is maddymara.com.

DRAGON GIRLS

**#1: Azmina the Gold
Glitter Dragon**

**#2: Willa the Silver
Glitter Dragon**

**#3: Naomi the Rainbow
Glitter Dragon**

**#4: Mei the Ruby
Treasure Dragon**

**#5: Aisha the Sapphire
Treasure Dragon**

**#6: Quinn the Jade
Treasure Dragon**

**#7: Rosie the
Twilight Dragon**

**#8: Phoebe the
Moonlight Dragon**

**#9: Stella the
Starlight Dragon**

**#10: Grace the
Cove Dragon**

**#11: Zoe the
Beach Dragon**

**#12: Sofia the
Lagoon Dragon**

Collect them all!

DRAGON GAMES

PLAY THE GAME. SAVE THE REALM.

READ ALL OF TEAM DRAGON'S ADVENTURES!

THE SPROUT FAIRIES

Forever Fairies

Forever fairies . . . and forever friends!

READ THEM ALL!